Angel
on the
Roof

Angel
on the
Roof

WALKER BOOKS
AND SUBSIDIARIES
LONDON · BOSTON · SYDNEY · AUCKLAND

Shirley Hughes

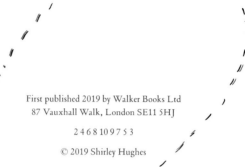

First published 2019 by Walker Books Ltd
87 Vauxhall Walk, London SE11 5HJ

2 4 6 8 10 9 7 5 3

This book has been typeset in Poliphilus

Printed in China

British Library Cataloguing in Publication Data: a catalogue
record for this book is available from the British Library

ISBN 978-1-4063-7964-8

www.walker.co.uk

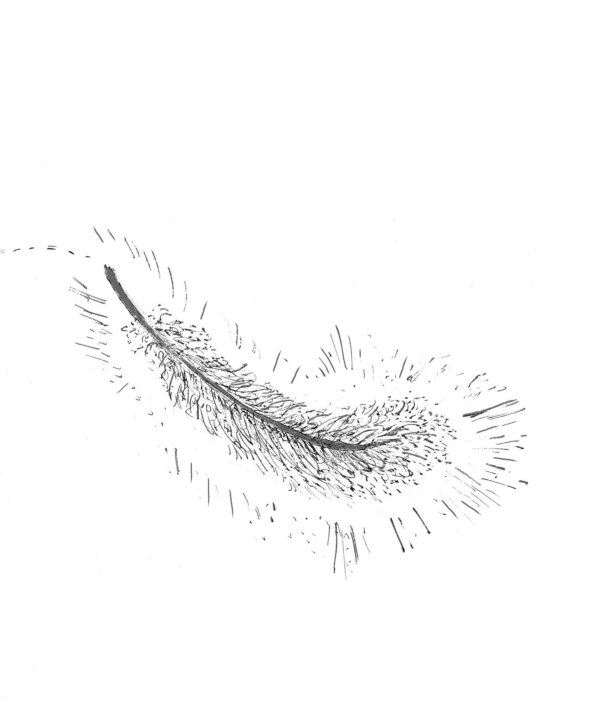

One bright moonlit night, an angel landed on the roof of Number 32 Paradise Street, just east of Ladbroke Grove in London's Notting Hill. He was attracted by the address. He had temporarily lost contact with base and needed to alight to give his wings a rest. He had flown over, but avoided, All Saints Road. Saints were in a different section where he came from.

Nobody noticed he was there. Mr Gantry, who lived alone on the top floor, heard some scratching noises but put it down to pigeons. The Sharples family, still awake, were too busy playing their radio very loud and shouting at each other to pay any attention. And Miss Babs Ridezski, who lived beneath them on the ground floor, was out at work, toiling long hours into the night as a hotel receptionist. Even if she had been at home she would have heard nothing. She had accustomed herself to sleep through anything.

Lewis Brown, who lived with his mum and dad in the basement flat, was too far down to notice.

The angel had come a long way and he was tired.
He folded himself into his wings and slept. When he
woke it was early, far too early for anyone in Paradise Street
to be up and about. Nobody saw him hop up onto the
chimney stack, spread his wings wide and give them
a good shake. He beat them briskly to
and fro. A golden feather fell out
and spiralled gently downwards.

Lewis Brown was the only person in the house who was awake. He was looking out of his barred basement window waiting for the day to begin. There wasn't much of a view. A brick wall, a glimpse of the street through the railings and legs hurrying past.

One of Lewis's legs was thinner than the other and not so strong. It bowed out a bit and made him slow getting up the basement steps. So he didn't go out much. He preferred to sit by his window watching people go by rather than hang about in the street, where the other boys might stare at him, or girls might giggle.

So it was Lewis who spotted the golden feather as it fluttered down and landed on his window sill. He unlocked the basement door and went outside to pick it up. It felt warm in his hand. He knew it wasn't a pigeon's feather or one from Mr Gantry's canary. Those were pearly grey or bright yellow and this one was shimmering gold, tinged with pink. Lewis tipped back his head and squinted up at the roof. The sun was coming up behind the chimneys. It caught something brilliant and alive, which trapped the rays and held them, pulsing so brightly that it made him blink.

He fetched the key to the main door of the house, slipped through the dim hall and climbed the stairs. He had to stop and rest his leg on every landing. At last, he reached the door that led to the roof, unbolted it and stepped out into the sunny morning.

The angel, who was sitting with his back to the chimney stack, stood up. His outline was slightly blurred, a little tentative, like a quick-pose life drawing. Light shimmered and whirred around his head. But the radiant smile was unmistakable. And that was the beginning of their great friendship.

Lewis spent hours that day, and the days that followed, talking to him. The angel did not have the power of speech, but he nodded and shrugged in all the right places. They sat on the roof as the sun edged overhead from morning into evening while Lewis, usually such a quiet, self-contained boy, fearlessly told him things he had never said to anyone before.

He talked about how he wished he could make friends more easily, and how miserable he felt when Dan Sharples turned up his music when they met on the stairs and pretended he didn't hear when Lewis said "Hello". And, worst of all, the boiling irritation he felt with his mum, who he loved, when she wore her anxious expression and urged him to go outside and play with the other boys. The angel took all this in, and much more, with his beautiful ears as transparent as glass and Lewis felt a lot better.

Lewis offered to bring the angel something to eat and drink, but he did not seem to need human nourishment. He liked just sitting and looking. He would keep quite still and gaze at the sky for hours at a time.

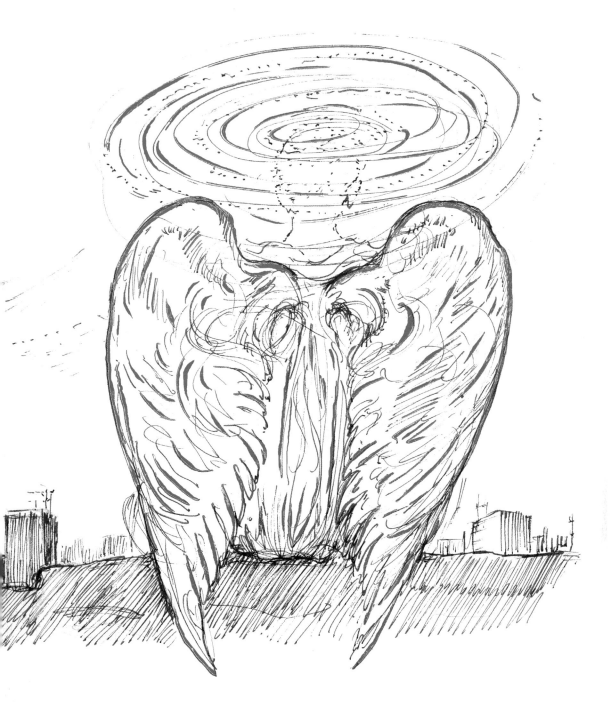

Lewis sat with him and gazed too. *Oh, that sky!* He felt he
was seeing it for the first time above the clogged city haze,
the trailing shape of clouds and the infinite variety of colour.

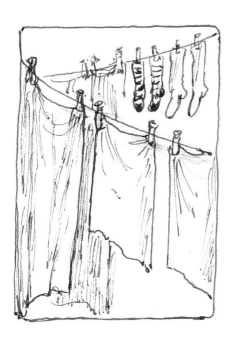

One day, Lewis fetched a baggy old overcoat belonging to his dad and put it on the angel to cover his wings. Together they descended from the rooftop and walked about the streets. The angel hardly seemed to notice the shop windows, but he liked to look up at the complicated outline of dormers, attics and crumbling cornices above and the skeletal arms of television aerials pointing heavenwards. He savoured the patterns of tall chimneys and washing hanging out and glimpses of people's lives through high windows. And he loved it when it rained.

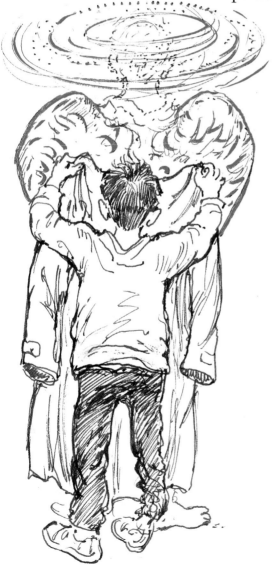

"Your friend got a bad back has he?" asked the boys who loitered outside the house. "Lewis Brown's going around with a hunchback now," they sniggered to one another. "Funny looking guy, isn't he?"

But Lewis's mum was delighted that he had made a friend. She knew from his face that he was happier and more complete in himself than he had been for a long time.

Things at Number 32 Paradise Street began to change. Nothing much to notice, only what might be expected with an angel on the roof. Mr Gantry seemed more cheerful, at least he did not grumble so much. Mr and Mrs Sharples went on shouting at each other, but their voices lost the jarring edge of anger. They even turned their radio down when Miss Ridezski was asleep. Lewis's mum and dad took to occasionally fetching canary food for Mr Gantry from the market. One evening they even asked him down to watch television with them.

And, most surprisingly, Lewis met Dan Sharples on the stairs without his headphones and they had a bit of a chat. He'd only worn the headphones all the time to block out the sound of his parents quarrelling.

It was the school holidays. Lewis spent a lot of his time up on the roof or wandering the streets with his new friend in the baggy overcoat.

Together they strolled slowly through the debris of the stalls when the market was closing down and, in the quiet evenings, among the discreetly grand houses on the higher slopes of Notting Hill, they looked in at the bosky gardens behind the iron railings. And all the time, an idea was growing in Lewis's mind. He thought and thought about it until at last he could not keep it to himself a minute longer.

He climbed the stairs and found the angel sitting as usual with his arms folded.

"You are my friend, aren't you?" Lewis blurted out. "My best friend – the best I ever had, aren't you?"

The angel held out his hand.

"You're an angel – you've got wings. You can do miracles if you want, can't you? I mean, like a real magician?" Lewis knelt down and put his face very near to the angel's and said in a low voice, "Will you do something for me? Will you make me strong and able to run fast? Will you do that for me?"

The angel simply sat in silence and held on to Lewis's hand.

"Please will you do it – please?" Lewis whispered.

The angel just looked at him, and it seemed to Lewis that he had become slightly transparent. Not only his ears, but his whole form started to fade.

After a while, Lewis let go of his hand and stood up.

"You can't do it, can you?" he said. "You can't do proper miracles. Or else you won't!" Then he turned away and walked to the top of the stairs. When he glanced back the angel was still in the same place, motionless by the chimney stack.

That night, Lewis was too miserable to sleep. He lay awake staring at his bedroom ceiling. Then he heard a tapping at the basement window. The angel was outside, strong and solid again, but now he gave off a silver glow like the moon. When Lewis joined him he knew something astonishing was going to happen.

The angel took him in his arms, spread his wings and up they flew into the warm night. *This must be a dream!* thought Lewis.

Together they swung out over the city towards
the River Thames, soaring above elegant cast iron
bridges, Gothic parliamentary pinnacles and huge
office blocks with endlessly glowing computer
screens. They flew over a great winking tower and
a mighty river barrier, towards mudflats and the
ever-widening estuary until they came to the sea.

Suddenly, the angel descended and Lewis felt himself drop from his grasp. He hit the water with a great splash and came up spluttering. But he wasn't in the least afraid. He lay on his back, carried on the swell, bobbing over the breakers, kicking up spray. And the angel flew just above him, dipping and hovering like a great seabird.

He was so happy and tired that he hardly noticed when the angel lifted him up, flew with him back to Number 32 Paradise Street and set him down, still dripping, on the roof. It was a wonderful night, the best of Lewis's life.

They stood together side by side and watched the sun come up behind the rooftops. When the first rays struck them, Lewis saw that there was only one shadow on the roof. The angel's body seemed to be melting into the sunshine.

"Don't leave me!" Lewis cried in alarm.

The angel merely smiled and took both his hands for a moment. Then he spread his wings and flew onto the chimney stack where he stood, poised. All at once, Lewis knew that nothing on earth would stop him from going.

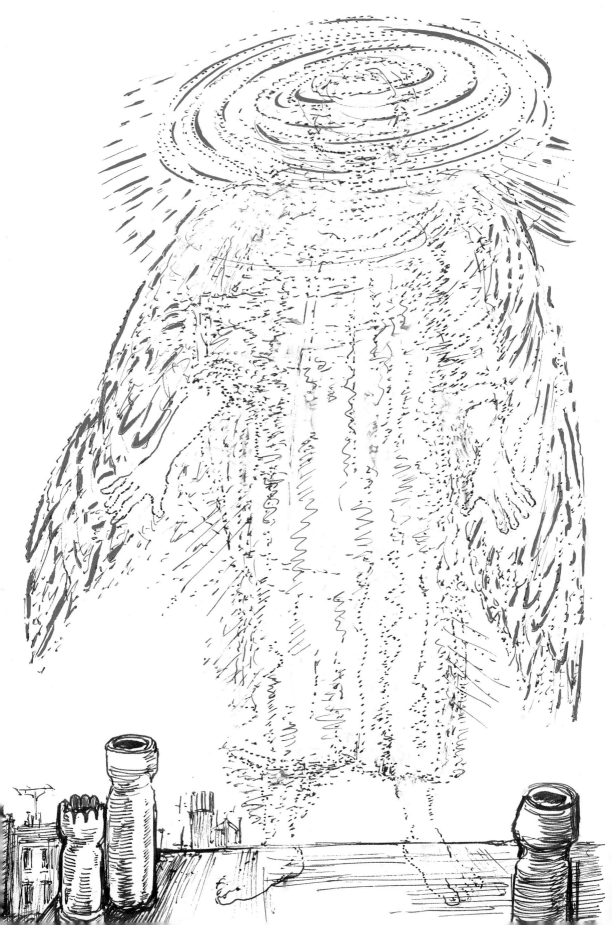

"Goodbye!" Lewis called bravely. Now the angel's wings were beating fast. He was brimful of light. "And thank you!" he shouted. "Thank you for…" His words trailed away as he saw his friend rise up in the air, hover a moment, then circle wide over Paradise Street.

He felt a rush of wings, glimpsed a pair of heels shooting heavenwards and then the angel was gone. Lewis blinked. His eyes were full of tears. He noticed his dad's old overcoat lying neatly folded on the tiles. He put it on and walked slowly downstairs.

Things continued to change a little every day at Number 32 Paradise Street. Lewis knew, although of course he told nobody, that some traces of the angel had been left behind. A less shrill feeling, some small kindnesses, an occasional unexplained waft of flowers on the stairs.

And once, in the quiet mid-afternoon, Miss Babs Ridezski started to sing in a high, yearning voice in a language they could not understand. Then, even the Sharples family switched off the radio to listen.

And Lewis had not forgotten how much he loved to swim. He and his new friend, Dan Sharples went to the swimming pool together two or three times a week, splashing and mucking around with everyone else.

Best of all, Lewis had not forgotten how to look,
which is how he started to become a painter.
And, years later, when he was grown up, people
took great pleasure in having their eyes opened by

his pictures: the skies and chimney pots, ebullient rooftops, sharp bird's-eye perspectives, the deeply etched shapes of old bicycles and airy flights of hung-out washing.

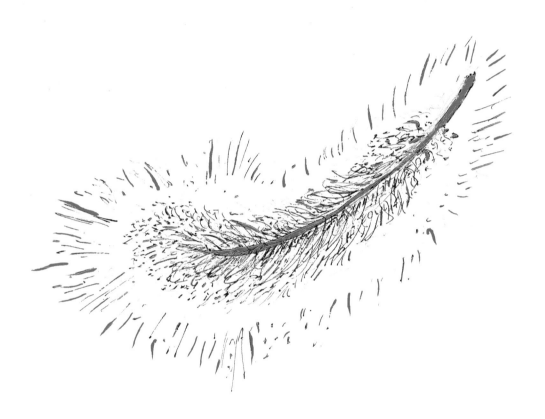

"That Lewis Brown paints like an angel," they said.

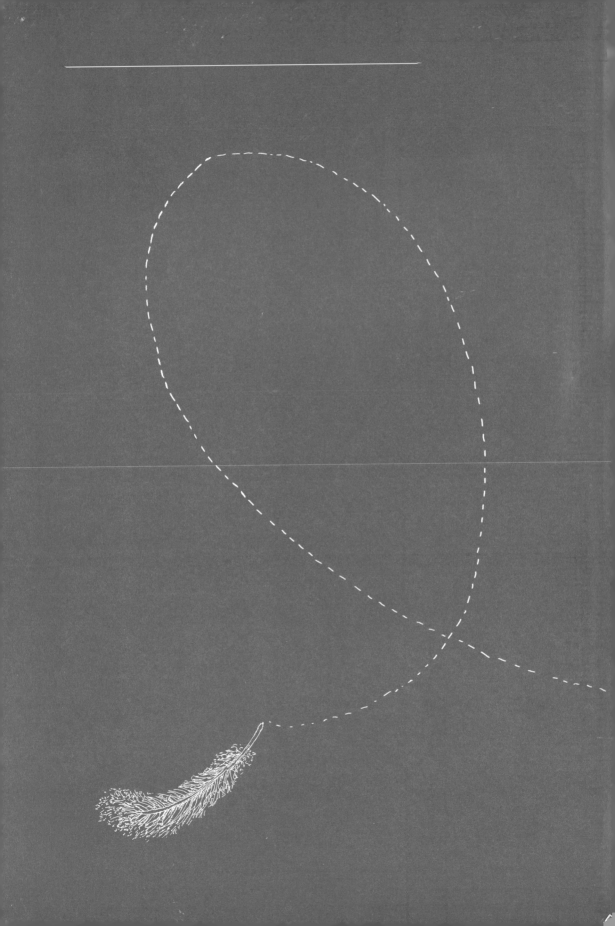